Disney presents

DOUG'S 1st MOVIE

CREATED BY
JIM JINKINS

Adapted by Nancy Krulik from a screenplay by Ken Scarborough

Illustrated by William Presing, Alisa Klayman, Brian Donnelly, and Tony Curanaj

Disney PRESS

New York

S.M.B.S.D. R.I.F.

SPECIAL EDITION

Original characters for "The Funnies" developed by Jim Jinkins and
Joe Aaron.

Printed in the United States of America.

First Edition
1 3 5 7 9 10 8 6 4 2

The text for this book is set in 16-point New Century Schoolbook.

Library of Congress Catalog Card Number: 98-88310

ISBN:0-7868-1401-2

For more Disney Press fun visit www.DisneyBooks.com.

Disney
presents
DOUG's
1st
MOVIE

CREATED BY
JIM JINKINS

Chapter One

Doug Funnie was not amused. He and Skeeter Valentine had been searching for the Lucky Duck Monster for months. But what he saw before him didn't scare him. He looked squarely into the creature's eyes and shouted, "Hold it!"

The monster jumped back and its rear end plowed into its front.

"You're not going anywhere!" Doug told the monster.

The monster reached its hands up and . . . pulled off its mask.

"Who's gonna stop us, Funnie?" Roger Klotz demanded. Roger and his gang were inside the monster costume. They grabbed Doug, stripped off his clothes, and left him in his underwear, trying to get his pants and sweater down from a tree.

Doug was furious. Roger was always goofing on him. But Roger was going to be sorry. One day Doug and his best human pal, Skeeter Valentine, were going to find the monster of Lucky Duck Lake. Then they would be heroes. And Roger would be exposed as the loser he really was!

Skeeter had no idea what had happened to Doug. He was busy searching the lake where a sewage pipe dripped. He heard a bubbling in the water and he fumbled for his camera. He leaned closer to the lake and suddenly . . .

"Roar!"

Skeeter snapped a picture in the direction of the sound. But as soon as the flash went off, Skeeter sighed with disappointment.

"Very funny, you guys," Skeeter told Roger and his friends, who were still in the monster suit. "You've had your fun. Now go home."

But Roger didn't move. He was frozen in fear. "Mon . . . mon . . . mon . . ." he stammered.

Skeeter stared into Roger's frightened eyes. "There's something bad behind me, isn't there?" he asked. Slowly, he turned and came face-to-face with a big, scaly lizard with sharp teeth.

"The monster!" Skeeter shouted, dropping his camera in surprise. *Flash!* The camera took a picture. The monster roared. Roger screamed like a girl.

Skeeter grabbed his camera and

grinned as he ran off behind Roger and his gang. Now everyone would have to believe him. There really was a monster in Lucky Duck Lake!

Chapter Two

As Skeeter and Doug left the photo store with Skeeter's developed photos in hand, Doug wondered if his best friend hadn't lost his mind.

"Skeet, are you really sure you saw something at the lake?" Doug asked gently. "I mean, you've been searching for this monster for months. You really wanted to see it. Maybe you saw a shadow or swamp gas or something. You do have a pretty active imagination."

6

Skeeter just gasped and handed Doug a picture.

"What's this?" Doug asked, looking at the giant webbed foot in the photograph. "Is this from your Halloween party?"

Skeeter shook his head. "It's the monster," he whispered.

Now it was Doug's turn to gasp.

"I told you there was a monster. I told everyone!" Skeeter shouted.

Doug grinned. "Skeeter, we're going to be famous! This is the biggest thing ever!"

Skeeter hoped that discovering the monster would make him an important member of the scientific community. Doug hoped finding the monster would make him important to Patti Mayonnaise. Lately, Patti had been spending all her free time with

upperclassman Guy Graham. She had even signed up to plan the school dance with him. Doug did not like that one bit.

Doug imagined himself as the great superhero Quailman! Only Quailman (and his trusted sidekick, Quaildog) would be able to save the dance from the attack of a scaly green monster. Patti would be so grateful!

Doug shook the fantasy from his eyes. This was no time for daydreaming. "Skeet, we've got to find that monster!" Doug declared.

That evening, Doug and Skeeter went back to the lake to get their bikes. *But their bikes were gone.*

"Where are they?" asked Doug. "They were right around here." Skeeter noticed some bike tracks leading away from the bushes. Alongside the tracks were big, webbed, monster-foot tracks. "Do you think the monster *ate* our bikes, man?" Skeeter asked Doug.

"Well, I don't think he's riding them around the bottom of the lake," Doug replied as the boys ran home.

"I was thinking," Skeeter said, as they turned the corner to his house. "If that thing ate our bikes, he might like cafeteria food."

Doug shook his head. "He didn't eat them," he said, pointing toward Skeeter's yard. The two bikes were standing there.

"I guess someone brought them back," Skeeter said.

"Yeah. Someone with monster feet." Doug gulped. He pointed to the huge monster tracks that led up the drive and toward the front door.

The monster was *inside* Skeeter's house!

Terrified, the boys gathered a welder's mask, trash can lids, tires, a rake, and a hubcap. They had their suits of armor. They were now prepared to do battle with the monster.

Skeeter turned on the light in the living room but when he walked by with his rake he knocked the lamp to the floor. *Crash!* The lights went out on the whole block. Doug volunteered to get a flashlight.

11

"That's okay," said Skeeter. "I know where it is."

"Oh no," said Doug. "I'm the guest. The guest always gets the spare flashlight. That's etiquette."

"All right," Skeeter sighed. "You win. Garage."

Skeeter made his way down the dark

hallway to his room. He tried to peek under his bed, but his armor suit made it impossible for him to bend. Then Skeeter heard someone enter the room.

"Check under the bed, wouldja?" he asked Doug. At least Skeeter *thought* he was talking to Doug, until he realized he was alone in his room with . . . THE MONSTER!

"Aaaaahhhh!"

As Skeeter yelled, his welding mask visor fell down over his eyes. He couldn't see. Skeeter yanked off the visor, threw it on the floor, and ran from the room.

The monster thought Skeeter had lost his head. He groaned sadly, picked up the visor, and cradled it in his arms. Skeeter watched him in amazement. Then he ran to find Doug.

"He's nice," Skeeter assured Doug as the boys went back to Skeeter's room. "He's not scary at all."

Doug and Skeeter watched as the monster picked up a book and opened the cover. "Wow! He can read!" Skeeter exclaimed.

But the monster wasn't interested in reading the book. He was interested in *eating* the book! He started chomping on chapter 3.

Forgetting his fear, Skeeter ran to the monster.

"Hey! This is a book!" he shouted. "You don't eat books! That's a no-no."

The monster cringed and looked sad. He reached out to pet the books.

"Wow," said Doug. "I think *you* scared *him*."

"I can't believe that. He tried to eat a book by Herman Melville," Skeeter said.

The monster looked at Skeeter. "I think he thinks that's his name," Doug whispered to Skeeter. Doug laughed. "Herman Melville—giant sea monster!"

The monster must have loved his new name. He raced over and gave Doug a bone-crushing hug.

Skeeter and Doug realized that this was a very big deal. It was too big for them to handle alone. It was time for Herman to meet Mayor Tippy Dink! She would know what to do to make them famous.

Chapter Three

Bud Dink, the mayor's husband, was surprised to come face-to-face with the legendary Monster of Lucky Duck Lake. In fact, it took the boys a while to coax him down from his safe perch high up in a tree. But when Mr. Dink finally climbed down, he wanted to call the Bluffington *Gazette* with the story.

His wife put a stop to the call.

"But Mayor Tippy, it's the story of the century," Doug argued.

"We have to think about what this story really means," she explained. "If your friend has been in the lake all these years, something must have driven him out."

"The lake is totally polluted," Doug explained.

"Exactly," Mayor Tippy agreed. "And who polluted it?"

"Bluffco Industries," Skeeter told her.

Tippy Dink nodded. "If we call the newspaper—owned by Bluffco—and tell them we've got a story that Bill Bluff is a polluter, someone will just kill the story. And that won't be good for Herman, either," she added.

"So you're saying we can't tell anybody?" Doug asked.

Mrs. Dink shook her head. "No. We just have to tell them in a way Mr.

Bluff can't stop. We have to call a city-wide press conference."

Doug grinned. A press conference. That would *really* impress Patti!

"Until then we can't tell anyone about Herman Melville—for *his* sake," Mayor Tippy continued. "I'll have the press come here tomorrow. Meanwhile, tonight, better keep him close by."

The closest place to hide Herman

was Doug's house. Doug figured Herman could sleep under his bed. He and Skeeter dressed Herman in Mr. Dink's old diving suit. Then they rushed him up to Doug's room. Doug's parents never suspected a thing. They thought Herman was Doug's sister Judy, in one of her drama club costumes.

But Doug's dog, Porkchop, knew better. He barked and growled at Herman. He did not want to share his room with a monster!

Doug took the squirming, barking Porkchop and deposited him outside.

"The one time in your life you decide to act like a real dog!" he exclaimed as he shut the door.

Skeeter agreed to stay overnight at Doug's to help keep an eye on Herman.

So Doug raced off to look for Patti. He found her planning the dance with Guy. Doug knew he couldn't tell Patti about Herman, but he wanted to make sure she was at the press conference.

"We have proof Mr. Bluff's polluting the lake," he told Patti. "It's going to be big news."

Patti was very impressed. So it seemed like a good time for Doug to make his exit. As he turned around, the photo of the monster's foot slipped out of his back pocket. Guy bent down and picked it up.

"I'll be right back," Guy told Patti as he tore the picture into little pieces. "Gotta make a call."

Chapter Four

The next day, before he left for school, Doug let Porkchop inside. Porkchop zoomed upstairs, barking frantically. He jumped up on the bed and stared the monster in the eye. Herman's face twisted. He looked angry. He reached down and . . . picked up a little heart-shaped piece of paper. He handed it to Porkchop. Herman loved Porkchop.

And from that moment on, Porkchop loved Herman, too.

After school, Doug was supposed to bring Herman to the press conference. But when Doug reached his block, he noticed a strange car parked in front of his house. And all of the neighbors seemed to be wearing dark sunglasses

and talking into their wristwatches. *Weird!*

Doug knew what he had to do. He took his place at the press conference microphone and nervously told the reporters, "I think we made a big mistake."

The reporters screamed out questions. But Doug didn't answer. He just watched sadly as Patti walked away— with Guy.

As the news crews packed their equipment, Skeeter and Mayor Tippy raced over to Doug.

"What's going on?" the mayor asked.

"Look," Doug said, pointing to the back of a TV truck. There was no news equipment inside. Instead there was a giant cage. Those reporters were really agents hired by Bill Bluff to capture Herman!

Obviously, Bill Bluff was more dangerous than any lake monster!

It was no longer safe to leave Herman alone. Doug was going to have to bring the monster to school with him. *But how?*

Doug dressed Herman in one of Tippy Dink's old dresses, put a wig on his head, and told everyone his new friend's name was Hermione.

Hermione was popular. Roger had a crush on her. He kept inviting her to the school dance. All Hermione did was grunt back at him.

Patti thought Hermione was Doug's new girlfriend. She was upset. Doug wanted to explain that Hermione was really the monster, but he couldn't.

Doug knew the masquerade couldn't work forever. So that night, he and

Skeeter went camping and took Herman back to the lake. They hoped he would go back underwater before Mr. Bluff got his hands on him.

As the boys and the monster reached

the lake, they were greeted with a foul smell. The water bubbled over with sludge. "I knew this lake was polluted, but not like this," Skeeter said sadly. "He can't go back in that lake, man."

"Then what are we going to do with him?" Doug asked.

"I think I can answer that." Bill Bluff's deep voice came from behind the bushes.

One of Mr. Bluff's men threw a net over Herman's head. Skeeter and Doug watched helplessly as the man gave Herman a tranquilizer shot and dragged him away.

"This won't be pretty for you," another of Mr. Bluff's assistants told the boys.

"I have friends at your school," Mr. Bluff threatened. "You boys could be in middle school for a long time. If you know what's good for you, you'll forget everything that happened here tonight."

But Doug and Skeeter knew they had to help Herman—*even* if it meant they would be in middle school for the rest of their lives.

"I just hope I don't have to keep taking band," Doug said as they ran back to town.

Chapter Five

That night Doug made a tough decision. He was going to ask Guy to help Herman. Guy was the editor of the school newspaper. *And* he claimed to know Bill Bluff. Maybe Guy could convince Mr. Bluff to turn Herman loose.

The next morning, Doug and Skeeter raced to the school newspaper office. They hoped Guy would be there, even though it was Saturday.

Guy wasn't in the office—but he had

been earlier. Doug could tell, because the computer was still on. There was a news story on the screen. The headline read: MONSTER DESTROYED!

Doug's heart sank. They were too late.

Skeeter read the article aloud. "A night of fun and enchantment turned into a night of terror for the students of Beebe Bluff Middle School when a horrific monster went on a rampage. At approximately 8:30 the monster burst onto the dance floor . . . "

That's when Doug realized the article was a fake. The dance wasn't until Saturday *night*. It was only Saturday morning. Guy had written the article before anything had happened. This was what was *going* to happen—that very night! Guy must be working for Mr. Bluff!

There was still time to save Herman. Doug and Skeeter tried to call Mayor Tippy but she was out of town. Who could help them? Doug dialed the phone and Al and Moo Sleech answered. Between the four of them they came up with a plan to save Herman.

Chapter Six

Funkytown was *the* place to be on Saturday night. All the kids were dancing. Patti was there with Guy.

Doug wanted to run over and explain things to her. But he couldn't even get close to her. Guy was keeping her to himself! Doug fumed.

Doug knew Mr. Bluff's men had hidden Herman somewhere. They were just waiting for the right time to turn him loose and kill him. That way it would look like they were protecting students, instead of protecting Mr. Bluff.

Doug spotted a giant heart right in the middle of the dance floor. It was big enough for a kid to hide in—or for a monster to *be* hidden in. Herman had to be inside the heart.

As Doug walked near the heart, he noticed it was cracking down the middle. Herman was trying to break free.

"No, Herman! Stay!" Doug ordered his monster pal.

Just then a loud commotion started on the other side of the room.

"ROAR!!!!" A large, scary monster bellowed as it staggered across the dance floor.

"*A monster! AAAAHHH!*" Kids were screaming and running in all directions.

Two of Mr. Bluff's special agents pulled out ray guns and blasted the monster in the chest!

The monster fell to the ground. One of the agents yanked at the monster's head and . . . whipped a monster mask from its face. It wasn't a monster. It was a robot, specially designed as a decoy by Al and Moo. The agents looked frantically around the room. Where was the *real* monster?

Doug yanked Herman across the dance floor and out the door. The agents didn't notice him because Doug had dressed him as Hermione.

"Hurry, Herman," Doug said as they raced toward the docks, where he and Skeeter had discovered a cleaner lake for Herman to live in.

Suddenly, Roger leaped from the darkness and blocked their path. "Out of the way, Funnie," he demanded. "Hermione, wanna dance?"

Skeeter raced down the dock. He yanked the wig from Herman's head.

"Aaaah! Lake monster! Gross!" Roger cried out.

Quickly, Herman, Skeeter, and Doug ran toward the lake. The agents and Mr. Bluff followed close behind.

Herman gave the boys a crushing hug. Then he dove into the icy water. He was free!

Mr. Bluff was not used to losing. As Herman swam away, Mr. Bluff threatened Doug and Skeeter, "I will dedicate every waking hour to making the rest of your days a living, pain-wracked nightmare . . . "

"Daddy!" Beebe cried. "Knock it off. Doug and Skeeter are my friends. Such as they are. If you have something to tell them, please discuss it with me."

"I think maybe you should discuss whatever you have to say with *me*," Mayor Tippy interrupted, as she walked onto the dock and stood beside Bill Bluff.

Meanwhile, the mayor told the kids to get back to the dance. It was cold out here on the docks!

Patti was standing on the dock. She was furious with Doug!

"I've been trying to call you," Doug assured her.

Patti wasn't buying it. Especially since Doug was holding Hermione's dress in his hand.

"Looks like you were busy," she said.

"This was what we disguised the monster in," he swore.

But Patti didn't respond. She just stared and pointed.

Doug turned around to find Herman.
The monster had come to say one last
good-bye. He held out a flower.

"Did you pick this for me?" Doug asked.

Herman shook his head.

"For Skeeter?" Doug asked.

Herman croaked out a single word. "Porkchop."

At the sound of his name, Porkchop burst out of the woods, ran up on the dock, and hugged his friend. Then, Herman leaped into the lake.

"I hope you like your new home," Skeeter shouted into the darkness.

Chapter Seven

Doug was just about to ask Patti to dance in the moonlight when Roger yanked him aside. "I just wanted to make sure nobody's gonna know I tried to dance with a *guy* monster," Roger begged.

"Your secret's safe with me," Doug assured him.

Doug was happy. He'd stood up to Mr. Bluff. He'd saved Herman. And he'd done the right thing—even though up until the last minute he was afraid Patti would think he was a loser.

"Well, maybe we should check out the dance, huh?" Doug asked Patti.

"Or not," Patti replied. "We can hear the music from here." Doug looked con-

fused but she held her arms out to dance—and they did dance, on the dock, in the moonlight.

"You think we'll ever see Herman again?" Patti asked Doug.

Doug saw a bubble in the water. Then he heard a loud "Glorb!"

Doug had a feeling Herman would be a part of their lives for a long time to come.